Anthony Patrick Jones, Jr.

THE LONE FEATHER

(Writings from the notebook of Vincent Oscar Raymond)

THE LONE FEATHER

PRODUCTIONS

THE LONE FEATHER

Anthony Patrick Jones, Jr.

FOR MY SON,

Gage Patrick O'Mara Jones

ACKNOWLEDGEMENTS

TO WHOM THAT IS CONCERNED, AND SUPPORTIVE: I am saying thank you for being there for me. I am also saying thank you to all those who have moved on. Without any of you, "The Lone Feather" would have a lesser purpose.

I thank the Almighty God, my Mother, my Father, Keisha, Danon, Melissa Monroe, everybody, and everything for making this memoir possible.

ልΨል

CHAPTER ONE

One Giant Leap for Man

1.

Living everyday with it

The weight on shoulders

Leaving it be

Wipe it away

To feel the sun on my face.

I sleep with an angel

Knowing that I can up and leave her

Just to get a drink of sweet water

ᎪᎠᎪ

Where are we going?

They all want me to change

But they can't see it now

That God has a plan for me

For this

Relishing time and falling out of sync

Living with it.

Don't cry for me when Tuesday comes

Try to remember the silly me

Once upon a time in life I was a King that had a soul

And spit at the feet of the god's just cause.

Now that I'm one of them I know where you live,

where you work, how often you pray, who you text.

Lord I can't watch anymore

ᎯᏇᎯ

Take these eyes

Beware, I too am thinking of a master race

To devour the ghetto fabulous

The lazy, the fat and nasty

The sky makes me strange

No more free hand outs

No more free lunch

No more food stamps

Even Ed Hardy is smart enough to perpetuate death

in fashion

Knowing all the time they'll immerse themselves

Chain themselves

Even hang themselves

For the nothingness praised

ΛΨΛ

Kiss kiss

Here is where fabulous gets very interesting.

Living everyday with shame if you are afraid

You should want it all.

2.

Spoiled by Jesus

A shadow of such

Still unknown to a particular mass as I leave it alone

Gone blank

Just to thank

Gage for being born

Stand up straight boy

And you will for as long as I breathe

ΛΨΛ

I'm no scarecrow

Keep your head out of the sand

Follow no gossip

All because there is no spoiling by Jesus here

This makes Jesus proud

Still unknown to a particular mass

So that I'll be proud of you

And if you don't have scissors to cut it

Tear it with your hands boy

Don't you dare whither in denial

Choose your voice?

Now smile at the world

To be amongst the fearless

And leave that spoiled by Jesus shit alone.

ᎪᏲᎪ

3.

Love got me drunk

But I have not forgot its promise

No shame

No shame

No shame

Hello

Goodbye

No shame.

4.

Since things happen to be working itself,

Towards a full circle

If Gina pops up

ᎠᏆᎠ

I see to it that I'll stay connected

She never knew what she meant

An imperfect love

Love I knew, needed, wanted

For a soul like my own

So run along children before lunch is no more

All things are possible, just be ready

When the second chance comes

Whoever you are.

5.

taste like chicken

feels like chicken

smells like chicken

ΛΨΛ

looks like chicken

moves like chicken

is this chicken?

yeah?

love yahl

6.

Dad told me not to run with those damned jackals

over that hill

I just needed

Wanted to hang

To know a new sport

Voices of Allah

Chanted bazaar rhymes

ΑΨΑ

Ghostly yet desperate

Up until I forgot mothers name

And any of the places I used to play

And whom I used to play with

I'd become

Loose yet more determined

I stayed hungry

Dad did not anticipate this

Or did he?

7.

What you don't see

Is how we all knew that night

Was our last night together

ᎠᏆᎠ

Yet there were enough grins and laughter to go
around.

It is all we ever knew

Ever known

About earth

We were walking away from everything that we've

ever known

Blindly into something new

However it tasted today, would not taste the same

come dawn.

Sounded like a service

However would it become a sin?

Far worse than wicked

Or the righteous thing to do?

ΑΨΑ

Selected for a new Gestapo

To clean

To rid

To lack remorse

Feared us all

However we clung together

Remembering,

Ben Neil

After the Gold Rush

Brought some to tears at times

It is all we had in order to green light us

This had to be done

With chaos

There is resistance

ᎪᎮᎪ

A resilience to survive

The lesser

The weaker

The ignorant

The selfish

The ungodly

Men

The pretender

The uncultured

The insensitive

Women

The superficial

The ghetto minded on all counts

No signs of intellect

ΑΨΑ

We killed it dead

In their homes

In their clubs

Children

On their blocks

In their churches

Elders

Etc…

Classified to no end

Operation rounded them up.

There are mass graves in 8 locals as far as West

Virginia

Painful enough

That no other man's say-so was behind it

ΑΨΑ

But our own collective reasoning at a chance for a
future
We've never had
Never would have
Unless
There would be a sacrifice
That would put Hitler's legacy to rest.
A voice like this
Ought be somewhat afraid to push these keys
But I push
So that you make sense of your own potential,
And quit blaming anything or everything and anyone
else
There is no current culture

ΑΨΑ

That says you are an intellectual ready for the world

Truth is that other cultures pity us

For not standing

Which is why we have a job

Despite the ills

I am only a GS-9 if it means much to you

What do you see?

We clean up our own mess

While you pray.

Dream on, your prayers don't make change

We do however

While you sleep.

Last we'll ask to you

Are we devils or trash men?

ᎪᎲᎪ

8.

As I look around and listen.

Not everyone that is born is to be wise.

That is where privilege comes into play.

As I look.

9.

I am no one but everyone.

I dream it as my neighbor

To be a part of something more

More than who we are and inspire to be.

So when I am called to approach the summit

I will be ready because of you

Whatever the want and what may come next. ... 2022

APA

10.

The world doesn't give enough love in return

That's Human error

The figure to blame.

I'm stepping out of my mind again to taste the

cheeks of Eve to rap with Adam.

God banging Mary and getting off without paying

child support, and leaving it to Joseph to marry her

Hell I see enough of that wackiness play out in your

everyday

Single women with kids

Wondering how do I fit into that

If I have to wonder in the first place

God is nothing but a pimp

ΛΨΛ

Without the fue,l the fire won't burn.

Giving babies out to the selected new Mary's

Even if now in the present day she can't conceive

that dude needs to be a father

She'll cling to her pimp

Her God

But I did promise myself when doc was digging and

pulling that bullet out of my chest while under

gunfire

That I'll love unconditionally till death even if the

imbecile has issue with it

Even with a mouth full of nuts and slob the odds

still weigh against your favor

So who's trifling?

ΛΨΛ

I have sympathy for Joseph
Considering how nothing has changed
Which is why "Doc" is still pulling that bullet out of
my chest even though I can't remember the first
name of that god.
The world doesn't give enough love in return
That's Human error.

11.
It is obvious that one thing has nothing to do with
the other but it is easy to summon conflict between
the two.
Be advised before jumping into any conclusion

ᎪᏇᎪ

It is more than often, that decisions make us bitter and unforgiving.

12.

Keep the Peace with self

Be real and true

With whatever U choose to do.

Keep the fires lit

So be it for Love.

Walk as often as U can

Just to reflect

How far U've come.

Cause if U come too close to Hell

I'll turn you around.

АРА

Love ain't for Suckas.
Yep.

13.
The sun is peeking
Bleeding through.
The squirrels are belly up
and I have all 30 of my kids today.
Life is getting better.
Simply better with each.

APA

CHAPTER TWO

Tea with Satan

14.

Then I was asked

Something bout Brothers today.

I said "Roughly it is in terms of desire and occupation in the millions. I take a slow and careful observation of the awareness and alertness of Cat's perspective of what life consists of. If being cute, too cool, looking for importance, or the lack of responsibility, minus

ΑΨΑ

their insecurities, despite however many are incarcerated versus living so-called freely, those numbers would easily exceed well into the millions. Millions.

There are not enough women to go around that understand the plight as a collective. Although women do outnumber men, not in terms of logic, but only in terms of rhetoric/fantasy, that is why so many men are in so-called Limbo. They largely put into perspective the need in order to maintain alone, so that she is not bothered by the struggle that suppress them as men. Clarity is all-most men seek, but many never reach, due to how they have been ignored. Music calms the

ᎠᏇᎠ

savage beast, and if they are considered Beasts, then it is music that is missing, imagine that. Survival it not the issue, but it is a matter of dwindling numbers, slowing approaching extinction, merely due to ignorance, and a particular need. Just take a closer look, and do the math."

15.

And the Lord spoke.

He said, "If I were to tell a joke now days, the self righteous being as anal retentive as many are, they simply wouldn't get it."

More of that wine "Please"

Sistah looks as if she needs Sum Luv'n...Hollah.

ᛉᛈᛉ

16.

Always an impromptu

Living in a sucka free nation

Strung out on mayonnaise sandwiches.

What exactly is the impugn

You ask.

Well each bullet is polished with spit only and blown

never to miss.

Ideal immolate

You can tell that I play poker with a hand full of

imps.

Rick James has blessed me with "Da Nasty."

Here is not quite the ode

However to have gotten out of bed

ΑΨΑ

To walk carefully into the backyard

Exhume someone that looked like Jesus

As I looked closely, he turned out to be my dad.

So I lay there with him until I fell asleep with him in

my arms

Melissa found me in the fetal position in the

backyard come morning.

Alone.

I am grateful that she is more than just a Christian

woman

More than a Woman is fair enough.

All because

Always an impromptu.

ΑΨΑ

17.

I am better at making mistakes

Than I am at being honest

Supply and demand dictates.

18.

Just before 4:10 a.m. I remembered

Everything is all right.

Move me, O' Lord.

It isn't easy to lead a spider when dancing; eight legs

to my two,

Quite a trip, I proceed.

Just before 4:10 a.m. I remembered.

Cake and candy for the party,

ΛΨΛ

Rain and Rainbows for cardholders,

808's and snares for those that came to dance,

Sushi and beef tender loin when they get hungry,

A bit of sake and honey wine for when we get
thirsty,

They are we.

19.

To lay with lilac,

To penetrate into reason,

To wrap my arms around another she devil,

Quite the hard on.

Skin like butter,

Surely makes a bro melt just thinkin bout it, bout it.

ΑΨΑ

No since in being coward,

Leave that to the public.

Still I'm tripping off of Mumbai,

The blood did flow,

Sad, sick, however brilliant.

One of these mornings to come I'm gonna spread

these wings and fly,

Where to,

That's uncertain.

However she's been an inspiration,

Behind my own brilliant chaos,

I could not have met her in church,

However I'll attend once a month with her,

Anything more than that,

ᎪᏔᎪ

It's just business.

I am no longer pacified by the shift in social ignorance,

I take the long way to work,

I take the long way home,

I just as well smack you in the way an SS Officer would a Jew.

For thinking that you're smart,

When all along I'm shadowing how you've broken my heart.

'You know who you are.'

There will not be a renaissance in 'Black Lit' without me,

Don't ask.

ΛΨΛ

Leave it be,

Thus leave it so.

These careless crafted tendencies,

Are not of a poets stretch,

Ole Iron Side said so.

So you can excuse me while I flip this ass over,

And tear into it 'DOGGIE STYLE' for a bit.

I at least enjoy being in my dreams alone,

Where friends are few,

And wild dogs roam many,

No misery,

Nor mystery at all,

However gravity is a tool that I use,

ΑΨΑ

And the difference between 'Save' and 'Slave' is the
'L'
But I use it for Love,
Even if it offends the Aloof.
To lay with lilac.
A gift to gab,
It was the year 2025 that I was designated for the
recovery of all toe tags in a mass grave unearthed in
Clinton, Maryland,
A cover up.
All victims were classified as John or Jane Doe,
How ironic,
All dates were from 2014,
All 214 victims were of African American descent,

ΛΨΛ

All men, women, and children,

From the age of 6 months to 74 years,

6 of which were pregnant,

All were of good health.

The numbers tell a tale all by themselves.

Brilliant chaos,

As an SS Officer would never mind a Jew,

Gravity,

Coward,

Savor the moment,

Savior,

Stay with me tonight,

Social,

Careless,

ΑΨΑ

To penetrate,

Not yet fully decomposed,

I don't recall doing this alone,

How am I associated to this?

I recognized 1 of my many chirography styles in a

suit jacket of one of the dead.

What else is hidden from me?

To lay with lilac.

20.

To all the Jihadist, and Uncle Sam's personal crusaders.

For the moment I am tired of all this death. Between

you both, slow your roll...please. No more soft targets,

where folks are innocent. If there is a beef with an itch

on the arm, do not scratch the leg, but scratch the arm, not the innocence of the public. Because between you both, God has nothing to do with what you are doing. Between you both, pick a battlefield and stay on it, until there is a last man, if any. Get your shit together, or the bleakness of tomorrow will be shared by you both. What a way to piss off God, if that is whom you both claim to serve.

Take a break from Death.

Men?

21.

Today is a day when we are to consider all the things to be thankful for.

ΛΨΛ

Family,

Health,

Shelter,

Stability,

To kindness from others and the kindness towards
those.

Today we are to consider how God has made it so,

To challenge our own regard to life.

Not just around the corner, or across town,

Even further than state lines.

We are to embrace this world of ours in a prayer,

In an effort to comfort,

To ease,

ΛΨΛ

Our own instability as Human and the mess we've made as a collective.

So I will atone this day and into the next for the world in which I live.

I will not rest until every square inch is covered both high and low,

Not until I've touched every cheek of both the young and the old,

The meek and the mean,

Until I am exhausted, with a love that can never be enough.

Today is a day when we are to consider all the things to be thankful for.

Happy Thanksgiving.

ΔΨΔ

22.

Tuscany, Italy calls,

To finish out my life and die there.

There is a strong conviction being tied to Colored

America,

Even if we've been colonized,

Been twisted,

Been bamboozled.

I love this cluster fuck,

Being able to lay low in a ghetto for a night,

Roaches and all,

Tucking toddlers in,

Then looking out from roof top to roof top,

And still dance with a senator's daughter the next.

ᎪᏆᎪ

You really don't wanna know what I love,

Nor how I love.

But then again I'm not gonna tell,

Not like this.

I will say that it's dangerous here,

How it has made me crazy,

I've done some unspeakable things,

However still enjoy having tea with Satan every

Wednesday like clockwork,

Because of the goody two-shoes,

Redemption is no personal crusade,

While hate is no friend of mine,

Nor an excuse,

Nor questionable,

ΑΨΑ

But you are free to keep guessing.

Tuscany, Italy calls.

23.

I was later told that I was clinically dead for seven

minutes.

But I swore that I and Gage where spending time on

a hillside having a bit of lunch.

Bite size roast beef sandwiches with orange soda.

After which tossing a Frisbee,

And sharing echoes,

Getting a kick out of the moments lost.

The day was perfect,

A perfect sky,

ΑΨΑ

Perfect wind,

Superb green grass that swayed as the wind could

only caress.

Even the sun hung in a perfect place.

Gage had grown and aged a bit,

Maybe I did too but just hadn't noticed.

We both were being silly.

I remember thinking how good it was being his dad

and how the moment was perfect.

Then I came to.

Back into the so called living,

Feeling as if I had been robbed of a perfect time

with my kid.

I wasn't done.

ΑΨΑ

24.

I wasn't suppose to say a word,

Nor help the dust to settle.

When they started speaking of soul train,

Ironically they all agreed on the lack of soul,

Today.

I was forced into priesthood,

Asked to keep writing it as I see it,

Feel it,

You need not question how,

I am you throughout,

Self-hate is a beast as it is,

But I'll lick its cheek if you are afraid.

In order to squash the thing,

ΑΨΑ

Know that you are going to kill it.

If you are going to debate it,

Know that I am due to sniff another line of blow,

Say fuck it!

And squash it for you,

Without breaking your balls over how slow you

move.

So sorry for not being a fag,

Though however when I open my closet,

There is a pile of corpses that reach the heavens in

there,

Because of my being a snail,

I'm getting comfortable at this,

From here to the Congo,

ΛΨΛ

From the Hill to the Vatican,

From the Shrimp Boat to South West,

From the down low to the hobo,

I'm but a small part in a massive factory working.

One's own convictions will always be challenged by

other's insecurities.

I wasn't suppose to say a word,

Freedom as well is that beast.

25.

I kept praying for less,

However this night carried me through.

All the evidence was against him,

ΑΨΑ

It was he that raped and murdered that little girl in
South East.

Some brother, it turned out to be.

So when asked rather I could,

I did,

Gutted him as some pig,

Made a mess of him.

I was carried through by his screams and jolts with
ease.

Still made it home at a reasonable hour,

To sleep as that little girl would have this night.

I kept praying for less.

I was only asked to do so,

Because I couldn't wait to do so.

☧

I kept praying for less,

And I'll do it again at a moment's notice,

Is this God's work?

Yep.

26.

No one man's burden is greater than another,

Since we all live here,

On this planet together.

One weakness is all ours to strengthen,

One strength is all ours to rejoice.

Together we all can make this work,

Despite our pride,

Despite how godless many appear.

ΔΨΔ

CHAPTER THREE

Ask Rufus

27.

It's not easy to imagine myself less of a Saint,

The humor slightly warped,

Though complex,

Humanist first,

A realist,

I must mention that the race pool must be

minimized.

ΑΨΑ

To redefine the gene pool, to put the imbeciles of

slavery brainwash to rest.

In a hole,

Moving right along towards a brighter plan,

Since there is no plan.

Fear and rhetoric being so,

So who will be the first to go?

This is of no responsibility to the Arian.

To intervene would be of fault,

So stand down, or we'll include the thing that you

hold dear and true.

Mind your business my cenacle friend,

Maybe we'll break bread in the end.

But first things first,

ΑΨΑ

I must mention that the race pool must be
minimized.
To redefine the gene pool, it's only entertainment.
Get a grip if you have a hard time imagining that
nigga is behind this,
I could be wasting a lot of time finger popping some
chick up against a wall,
Until she cums into my hand,
Yet still be willing to taste her nectar,
She wants to, from these fingertips.
Isn't life grand?
It's not easy to imagine myself less of a Saint,
however, it's only entertainment.

ΑΨΑ

28.

Either way isn't safe, so if we're gonna do it,

Go fearless with it,

Hell I figure that there is only one way out of this

madness.

So listen carefully,

Do what I ask of you and you'll make it through this.

Put the fear aside or use it,

I'm gonna get you out of this.

Ok.

29.

She's like a piece of cake,

That I had when I was seven,

ΔΨΔ

My own very slice of heaven,

And all I really know for sure,

Is how to love her.

I love her.

30.

I only serve one master,

I am in it,

But not of it.

We do take this seriously,

So if you move or utter a word,

I will shoot you in the face myself.

Otherwise you'll see the sun tomorrow.

Do I make myself clear?

ΑΨΑ

I do not mind making a river of this.

I'm already loved

So let us redefine cool.

31.

To drive into black water,

To recall,

To dig into it,

Without remorse,

To feed the pestilence to the dogs,

In order to rejoice,

Life isn't a joke,

And still you piss you off.

Where is the great evil coming from?

ΛΨΛ

And how do I kill it?

Keep the truth simple.

Grab the keys to the truck,

To recall,

To drive into black water.

32.

In Jesus name.

First they had the nerve to separate using race,

Then they had the nerve to separate using degrees

and experience as leverage,

And it's working just fine considering how well many

mimic,

Do as you are told!

ᎪᎨᎪ

What's next takes a bit of imagination,

To split the Black Church into pieces,

The posers do take up a lot of space.

In Jesus name will take on a new meaning,

and for those that want to sit on their fat asses, wait

and do nothing,

Will be those left like lambs for the slaughter.

To break bread with saints again is no little boys or

girls dream.

Instead they are groomed to play safe and imagine

secular objects,

Into teens,

Girls hugged up with girls,

Boys into little fags,

ᎪᏪᎪ

A walk through the mall is what it is,

All the while the parents condone,

Pretend not to see.

Not swords and shields.

Nothing like Lil Billy, the son of a red neck,

Who learns to hunt and fish with skill and still

attends school in the city.

The Church will split,

In Jesus name will take on a new (meaning),

But first they had the nerve.

33.

Never mind my condition,

I make sure I take my medication.

ΛΨΛ

When I feel like.

What I gather is illusive,

What scorns me is lucid.

I enjoy the shakes and the voices,

The noises the house makes as it settles,

I'm never alone,

Someone or something sees to that.

If it weren't for the girl,

Love would have been the train passing the station,

A blur in the night.

She's unusual.

We all are aware the toll that their conflict has on us,

The isolation that back-wash can't deal with,

It isn't their fault,

ΛΨΛ

They are merely serving their civic duties,

Full of questions but no conclusive answers.

Look for the following in the weeks to come.

A smile,

Mom,

Hog,

Papa,

Oven,

Organ,

Lip,

And a kid named "Joey" that just got back.

There are neither shadows nor underground,

Keep things as they are, in plain sight.

The truth is how well we all pretend simultaneously.

ΛΨΛ

Juicy steak, drink in hand, girls on the beach.

Shhhhhiiit....

Lil Black Hitler working for the State Department,

That's funny,

I can see his bowl of lollipops on his desk now.

Who would have perceived him to being a closet

AC/DC fan?

Those were the days huh.

I should really go take my meds.

Watch your six.

34.

Without a Lil Red Meat or Squirrel in your diet, then
you are nothing but a Scaredy Cat.

ᎠᏫᎠ

Country boy has a green light at monitoring the fat around the gut; it'll keep NSA busy.

Happy Birth Day "Fat Head"

35.

I can admit that I am not the nicest guy in the room at times,

Not surprised at all.

We as Humans are making this entire thing up day by day,

It tastes like wishful thinking.

She is safe believing in rules,

While I beg to differ.

There are no rules.

ᎪᎾᎪ

Safety isn't safe at all.

In fact the idea of safety that is dictated generates more fear and instability for the entire world.

I've changed my mind.

In fact so that the so called terrorist is nothing more than a freedom fighter protecting their own way of life.

Devoted to God, not disillusioned by freedom.

The Negros in America ought to know better,

Considering how they came into bondage in the first place.

Now the village has decayed,

An 11-year-old child has hung itself, because my idea of safe has you devoted to my way of living.

ᎪᏇᎪ

That really isn't safe for you at all, not for you.

Only mankind.

I have my God,

My freedom,

I can snatch your ass up,

Torture you for sport,

Kill your safe ass, and move on.

Remember the Atlanta Child Murders?

It was me.

By the likes of your everyday conversation you've

forgotten "The Summer of 79."

I can admit that I am not the nicest guy in the room

at times,

But I know the reason why I am here.

ΛΨΛ

Then I was asked what do I prefer.

Wishes for wolves or witches while assuming never knowing which is which.

Guess my answer.

Once in the system it has a way of not allowing you to move on,

As to,

The right to being a patriot is only reserved for the privileged.

But however the sound of rebel and eggshells beneath my feet,

I make it a point to let you know that I'm coming.

Who tip toes anymore?

ΛΨΛ

Now you know, that I don't do this for recognition, art or the imagination.

For what purpose?

I may be apt to tell you, only if you bring the gravy for the mashed potatoes.

So before I go nowhere fast,

I'll pause,

Pay a bill, and leave the earth to continue to orbit,

Before I say "Fuck it!", and spin into another direction,

Leaving your jaw to drop, because this ain't Neo Soul.

There is a data trail for those that understand 1984, those that have seen the film.

ΑΨΑ

God is something else,

Something dangerous,

Not nearly as safe as a newborn.

I wanted to be here, even though,

I can admit that I am not the nicest guy in the room

at times.

36.

When little sister,

For a chance again to be safe with a shelter.

A place where no man can come and take us away.

When little sister,

My eyes also need to see, Joy seized.

ΔΨΔ

It is the lack of interest that can cause others to get
hurt.

Even in the work place.

I had a sit down with a few new saints.

The stakes have been raised even higher,

It may very-well be a set up, a trap.

When the people throughout the land have needed
for far too long now.

There will be a shift in a chain of events,

Once in office.

The People will still hurt and grow restless, and
spiteful.

And someone is going to get hurt.

Let's keep in mind that this is America.

ᎪᏇᎪ

The fool easily nation.

Be aware.

OH! When little sister,

Because! My eyes also need to see,

Joy seized.

37.

I have sold my soul,

Yet still I am my mother's son,

Both are a worthy reward.

I am known as a monster,

But only by the liar and the taker,

Because they can't have their way.

I can be still in the darkness,

ΑΨΑ

Eat your sins whole,

And hold back the vomit until I've left you.

It's the hustle,

The food on the table, the bills paid,

The Christ that I've resurrected from,

While lurking in this day and age.

I have sold my soul.

38.

While on the ladder,

Practice mastering,

Serve a situation that is constantly developing the

Human intent.

Self-destruction is not an option,

ΔΨΔ

Here is a new contraption.

Love isn't blind at all,

Though someone said it was.

Less stress when you are infamous,

Once famous, you can never go back.

So choose your move wisely lad.

But what if I said, "The past can be changed."

And that I will not be willing to discuss it nor debate it.

Where will that leave us?

On a beach during high tide,

Or in a stairwell that reeks of piss heated by the heat of summer time.

ΛΨΛ

For these breadcrumbs are not laid for this

generation,

But for my sons, and those still in diapers.

Here is a new contraption.

Be that lion, and every move that follows,

Frame for frame,

Even slow the motion.

From the reach to the bring down.

Beast for beast.

Mothers show your daughters,

Fathers show your sons,

Blissful perfection is every beast's needs, in order to

survive.

This is not "Black Literature", only literature.

ΑΨΑ

As in for example, "If you don't eat your meat you
can't have any pudding." … Pink Floyd.
So don't worry the little hairs on your head,
Grow up,
It's not you that I fall asleep each night beside.
I am secure.
While on the ladder,
Have fun,
Pure fun.

39.
What of the set up,
What of the Saint,
What of the rapture,

ΛΨΛ

That I participate.

Immoral notice,

Immortal for sure.

You can't reason with all beasts,

Though there is an urge to kill them all.

Shut dem Niggas up, give them a black president so,

we can move on.

Roger that,

One Black President so that we can move on,

To close that chapter.......................over.

What of the set up.

If that is all that it takes to make their Black assess

feel better, they could have put one of their own on

the moon.

ΛΨΛ

For their resources aren't limited,

Looking for a hand out still.

So who's dancing the two-step now?

Ah, all I can say is, "That's why we pay Lil Wayne."

For even the walls and the hallways of the Vatican
would plant a seed of fear,

Deep into him.

He knows that he's not welcome here.

Tis the very reason why I don't bother to recycle,
trash begets trash, while I concentrate on other
things.

What of the set up.

CHAPTER FOUR

New Keys and Gate Keepers

40.

Don't' move me Baby,

While the pictures are burning,

Steady Mate,

As we approach from the blind side.

One less reason to plant squash this year,

Consider it bad news,

As I debrief my peers.

ል૱ል

In order to confirm,

There is an impulse.

A railway into reverse psychology, Out of control,

Little concern to you,

And I wouldn't think twice about it,

If you were me.

I'm in the paint,

Ice cream cools this Nigga down.

Foreign dialogue is in which?

To know what of the which,

Not just any witch.

Dripped over the Big Dipper tonight,

And laid there for awhile,

To think,

ΑΨΑ

And to be as we wish which.

Never the mine,

Never mind,

Still building that spacecraft out back.

Slowed down once before,

Tied too loose is the knot,

Tea with Satan tomorrow,

Need someone to talk with.

Gina is no longer,

Space makes it so,

A bitter forgiveness is proper amongst my kind.

We adjust this way,

To make room for the next,

Make sense,

ΑΨΑ

Since it doesn't make any sense,

Of what makes sense,

Which is witch?

Lay down the dust,

Duh Country or D.C.

Too easy to fit in,

Witch not wish,

Which is witch?

The pastor asked,

And I in turn answered fair,

Not at all careful,

Though true.

I've come to Love this of which,

Which to belong is fair,

ΛΨΛ

Ever which witch.

Has some sense of logic,

And this should be less complicated all because of

English.

Condemned,

I very well maybe.

I sweat not.

In order to confirm.

The goof ball knows nothing of the village,

Nor the struggles to fortify it,

and keep it in tact,

Neither the sacrifice,

Nor the security of the bloodline,

Nonnegotiable.

ΔΨΔ

To behave as a crab in the basket,

You will be banished for your selfish ways,

Without access to the fruits of our labor.

Heed these words of the Lord.

That whomsoever shall be banished, and tries to

return into the fold,

Shall be cut down in the very place that they may

stand.

A warm walk through 65,

An unexpected outcome.

41.

It's a half moon tonight,

All things about the day have gone right.

ΛΨΛ

So I'll sleep tight.

It's a half moon tonight.

42.

Switching Roles:

More Masculine than Feminine.

More Feminine than Masculine.

Women Cops:

The stress of the Bread Winner.

Over 40 and no Kids.

Missing Children.

Dress Code versus Mind Code.

Rapture or Revolt.

ΛΨΛ

First Generation Wealth.

Birth Control.

The Courage to Lead.

Suicide or the willingness to Die.

The connect to the Cage.

The connect with Freedom.

Black Love Unique.

Coping with Genocide.

True sorrow for the Sparrow hides in Scotland Yard.

Arrogances before the Hunt.

Should I cry for you?

I'd die before knowing.

Jim Crow Jr.

ΛΨΛ

Aryan Nation Insignias in Fashion / What are Black
Youth wearing on their backs.

Pull your pants up son.

What is Black Music?

What village.

Resisting Companionship.

Exploring the Book of Revelation.

How to get rid of Black Men.

How to pacify Black Women.

The Plot to destroy them Both.

How to stick Together.

Playing Ignoramus.

Ignoring the warrior.

The Art of Passive Aggression.

ΑΨΑ

Who'll Kill Cain?

The Blueprint to saving a Few.

The Ultra man Clan.

Tell me that you love me.

Not another Freak'n Tattoo.

Math.

Peanut Butter and Jelly.

43.

Linda and I didn't have kids; we had Lindsey, our pet dog as our child for 10 years now. Until the cancer hit Lindsey we believed that we were fair parents, I still struggle with it. Treating the cancer cost as it would for a small child, and the stress to save a life took its toll

ΑΨΑ

on my very soul, disillusioned, had we lost it? Throughout the chemotherapy Linda and I prayed for Lindsey's life, for Lindsey's health back.

Then I had a dream one night while driving on a back road through the dark, no rush while Linda lay resting with her hand lying on my lap. I began to break as a sharp curve approached, then from out of nowhere, I saw what looked like Lindsey dart into the lane, passenger side, and just as I began to swerve, simultaneously an Amish boy ran into the road, driver side.

ΔΨΔ

I have ruined my choices; as the kid looked in my face through the high beams, just as I was closing my eyes to brace his impact, heard him pass beneath the car. I knew that it was God, smiting Linda and I for our efforts to save a dog, a fuckin dog bottom line. Any child deserved that same love, we've made that choice. Lindsey died that same morning, when I awoke to the call from the vet. ... Fin

44.

So what that I've learned to love at the expense of the unfamiliar.

Don't wanna own or be owned,

Don't wanna date,

ΛΨΛ

If you have other plans,

Rather in need of a friend,

Than a husband to suit an unwarranted need.

And all the fraud that follows as a product of the

status quo, cuz they ain't happy you dig.

They've dug themselves a trap that even the pastor

can't resolve.

So what that I've learned to love.

45.

For I know that He my son be it a lil rogue,

Though however He serves me well in His ways.

Thus may you learn from Him.

For He is Me,

ᎪᎽᎪ

Already been you.

He'd bleed for you,

He'd die for you,

But you'd not for Me nor He,

As He would,

As He prepares.

46.

Bu'ga Soup.

Got'cha

47.

When I grow up,

I want to look back over the years,

አፃ

and praise the marvel of a garden I've given,
Unto this.

48.
Whenever God is pleased,
So am I.
However on the days that God isn't,
Neither am I.

49.
I'm not going to concentrate on rather or not I'm
evil or divine.
I do know for sure that I do want to be the last in
line.

ΛΨΛ

50.

You see, even as a teen I was happy. The same kid that could pull out his eyes, and Rip away the flesh from his face, and still go long to catch the winning touchdown, during the street ball years. All because of Lynn Swann. You see, I'm still that kid.
Happy.

51.

It dawned on me this morning, while sitting on the toilet, taking my morning POOP, having my morning CIG, and morning JAVA, that I hadn't cried in a very long time, too busy I guess. I think it's gonna come out

ΔΨΔ

after my son's vacation with me is over. I'm due for tears.

You can be strong without being insensitive.

Silly Me. … Peace Yahl.

52.

What happens when it doesn't hurt anymore?

When the grace that we all seek is no longer out of reach,

Achievable.

I have laid low in this river of pestilence long enough,

Counting those that bring shame upon a legacy of tears, blood, and bone.

ᎪᏌᎪ

Thus the aim for the remaining few must not claim

themselves victims of circumstance nor religion.

From now on those that can understand this,

Your life is in my hands, so that mine be in yours.

I realize what I don't know,

Yet make believe is but a tease,

Love dwells in a galaxy too far away to see,

While I am able to still find joy in the sometime,

Yes I say only sometime.

I say that it is useless to criticize my neighbor,

When my own house is in disarray.

Racism is a distraction,

Gay power is none of my business,

OK ALREADY ON TO THE NEXT.

ΑΨΑ

I applaud them all for their contribution to the world
of confusion,
Is that what they are so proud of?
So what really happens when it doesn't hurt
anymore!
Even when I had fallen, and the dogs started to bite,
Ripping away my garments, tasting my blood,
chewing my flesh,
I was still in heaven even after the Billy clubs and
boots got their piece,
LET IT FLOW!
Those Alabaman cops surely made me feel
comfortable.

ΛΨΛ

When just a slight turn connects me with the warmth
of the sun on my cheek just right.
Know that all of you have contributed to what I am
today,
And it doesn't hurt anymore.

ΑΨΑ

CHAPTER FIVE

A Slice of Orange "Please"

53.

If you believe that God is so Patient.

The question is will God then Hesitate.

At the expense of the Human.

Patient versus Hesitate.

What is it of God?

What is it you believe?

Sucka.

ΑΨΑ

54.

Without the Arts,

There would be no images in the mirror.

No joys or horrors,

No Heaven nor Hell to predict.

Nothing at all to grow upon.

No devices,

No dreams.

No knowledge of how to mimic God,

Not even for a day.

Without the Arts.

God's chosen few would not have a clue, of the
Voodoo that we do just to keep the mirror full.

ΛΨΛ

Nor have a clue of the sacrifices into hell we've made, lingered, been trapped, have stayed, and have fallen.

In order to secure a simple truth of the Goodness that comes out of creating creation.

Silent conversation with God, Ambassadors first before others.

We are not as sensitive as you think,

We are saving souls without saying so.

We are as gods.

Support the Arts.

55.

The step into,

ᎪᎹᎪ

She wanted fish for dinner,

Awoke sweating again; being chased or running after something.

The step into.

The days quiet time,

Lap over the sounds of fowl and of occasional traffic gone by.

My for the moment backing track,

A muse,

A world without rules can only mean chaos, she said.

Don't be fooled by rules, I mumbled under my breath.

Never mind,

Into the step,

ᎯᏇᎯ

The step into.

She's cool.

56.

Can't eat,

Can't sleep,

Can't look my Lady in the eye,

Can't play with our child.

Can't do my job.

Because of what I saw.

Started out a good day,

All intact,

Home was golden,

Before I left.

ΛΨΛ

For a walk through Fort DuPont Park.

Over the hills and through the woods,

Refreshed,

From the week.

Maybe I'll fire up the grill,

Or even tinker around.

I was chill'n.

Until I saw a small sneaker,

Then a small sock nearby,

It was no surprise,

That it began to blow my high.

Not even for a second,

Before taking it all in.

AΨA

There it loomed in an old creek bed that I used to
run with childhood friends.

A little boy,

Laid like garbage,

Grew so quiet all around,

The chill from out of nowhere,

The vomit I surrendered to,

The age that could have been,

A darker side of living.

Underwear tied around

Throat and left arm.

Decay,

Butt-naked,

For a walk through Fort DuPont Park.

ᎪᏇᎪ

Right now,

I just can't.

57.

Remembering "Peacfo"

UHMM…

58.

Again it was that place,

Remembered as the last.

Nothing has changed since.

Every stone in its place,

Every cloud,

Every tree,

ᎪᏫᎪ

Even every ripple on the lake,

Was in turn to the other.

It is here that the Lord has given me a place to keep.

Again it is that place.

59.

If you can handle the fragile,

You can handle anything.

60.

Input:

Encourage steadily.

Constantly explore the child's creative mind side.

Develop their self worth, their self esteem.

ᎦᏆᎦ

Maintain open dialogue with their interest in mind.

Introduce and maintain outside of the box thinking.

Allow them to develop their own interest along with standard curriculum.

Reframe from the status quo approach to learning.

Use their influences to strengthen their so-called learning weaknesses.

There are several paths towards educating youth, but if the end result is without reward for the educator, and the student, the wrong path has been chosen.

Consider exploring:

Bach etc

ΑΨΑ

Einstein etc

Miles Davis etc

Robert Frost etc

Cornel West etc

NASA

Philosophy

Japanese Culture etc

Politics

Tai Chi during gym

Banking

Bill Gates etc

Photography

Jean-Michel Basquiat etc

ΛΨΛ

Change their entire perspective of role models, and replace them with other influential entities. It takes a pioneering spirit to educate a child into someone new, someone influential that the world can applaud.

Body:

The very question we must ask ourselves, is how are we to educate, and if the current approach is working. Are we to conform, or to build onto? Is it for all, or the selected? Is it equal or segregated? And last, why do some parents prefer veggie dogs over beef, pork, chicken, or combination hot dogs, and does this decision making factor into education, and if so, then why?

ᎪᏔᎪ

I have dutifully noted through experienced observation that the self-esteem issue starts at the parenting level, rather low, sufficient, or rarely superior. So-called African Americans are what they mimic, usually through media or continental influences, otherwise to assimilate. Another question is if the African American has an identity, or are they struggling with it? Why don't they feel privileged, while other nationalities and cultures use it to their advantage? So-called African Americans are mixed with some other race, customs, culture, heritage, and don't even know it, or explore it.

This is where their entire world is set in the linear perspective, one sided, from the cradle to the grave.

ΑΨΑ

Not to mention that somewhere in between the notion of banking on Jesus to save them comes into play. This alone takes away from self-reliance, self-preservation, self-assurance, in tales creates more room for selfishness, particular insecurities, and self hate, all due to not being educated any differently, or not having that opportunity in the classroom.

If it is a matter of race, then so be it, if it is a matter of class, then so be it, and if it is a matter of survival, then continue to discuss it. Consider that being content is no longer an option, nor that any civilized country can benefit from foolish pride without feeling the repercussions of its own instability ignored, sooner or later, history dictates this. It is not easy for me to consider weighing in on this issue of importance, that all are to benefit from, tricky topic nonetheless, however crucial. I've faced particular challenges, handed down from one generation to the next, to conclude that life, just wouldn't be the same without them, and that there is a point somewhat to this.

Caring has been the greatest blessing for sure, playing a role of influence, a small role, because of the bigger picture of being human, and to understand the privilege of the communal experience, the rest is easy, and it can be taught.

ΛΨΛ

I thank you for this opportunity, being able to express some thought into a legitimate concern. To all that do care enough to ask the question, and to those that do care to answer. I applaud you all, and wish you the best in this endeavor.

Sincerely,

Anthony P. Jones II

Thank you for asking the right question. It again has been an Honor and a Privilege.

61.

The Glory that I sought in those days was not the glory of men.

ΑΨΔ

And to pity them would have been the death of me
and all those who cared.

We purified our own race, so that we would survive
the future.

62.

You are a part of this, just like I am.

Memoirs of a secret empire,

Warriors of God only,

Sleeps with death,

Comforted by a woman that understands this aspect
of God that the rest can't stomach.

Environments or genetics,

Something else or mental illness,

ΛΨΛ

An experience that supports yours,

Change is the watchword for childhood,

Once cute,

To gone sad,

Fooled you really, just to get you,

Stayed humble all along,

My story hasn't been told; been teaching you all

along,

Changed my mind as a child,

Tweaked combinations very young,

Made to be very human,

I am at risk of your waste,

Laid back in your face,

Not bitter, though dutifully noted.

ᎪᏇᎪ

Survival before religion,

Am I saved?

Or am I praying to be.

Get a bloody nose whenever I think about it.

So I do; So I don't.

I stay interested.

Even while other's confidence go.

63.

I don't imagine,

I don't care,

I am envied,

While contemplation to worry.

"How do I do it?"

ΑΨΑ

"How do you do it?"

I often find myself behind the quarter.

Where is the draft coming from?

Too lucid to wish for anything.

The season for my caring goes undisguised, even

unasked.

I don't imagine,

I don't care,

I am envied,

I do see the fine,

Savor the fruit,

Watch the skyline,

Kiss, drink and dance,

While some call this sin.

ΛΨΛ

I do not wander,

I do not fear,

I do not hesitate,

I don't want to be your man,

I don't want to be your friend,

I do not want to be anything,

That you cannot comprehend.

The collective soul is of more value than one,

One soul at fault, is all at fault.

And as I look into my rear view mirror, and see her

resting back there,

Another hit would make sense as I lean into the next

line.

Blow back the white sheets,

ΑΨΑ

Meet me again on the trail of tears,

Reminisce over the Holy Ghost in that small

backwoods sanctuary,

Rather be important, even famous is your

importance,

Watch your own steps, rather than mine.

This is far too easy; nothing laid here is on the line,

The words are blurred for sure, only because you've

made them so,

Although clear.

I don't imagine,

I don't care,

I am envied.

Fin. 08

64.

"I have that already, and plus it got back to me that I wasn't "Black" enough." What they meant was, is that I've minimized my grief, that they can't understand how so. "I'm cool with that."

65.

Even if the things we thought that we believed in, versus what we are made to believe all changed in an instant. What would come of us, you, or other things? For example, if Jesus was merely only born out of wedlock and no other way, would it change your belief in the man? Joseph the single Father of Christ is no different than the millions of others throughout time,

ΑΨΑ

including myself. At least I can come to terms with the way in which Joseph's role compares to the present. History may have written Joseph off for a reason, considering how single Mothers are more forced into raising their sons, while they juggle far more than they can handle.

Did Joseph pay child support? And if so what sort of arrangement was made, between him and Mary. But anyway, as I said earlier, "If Jesus was born out of wedlock would it change your perception of the faith you have already put into the man." Yes or No.

66.

Lord you know that I'll be first to tell you,

ΑΨΑ

"You got jokes."

I can keep it ashy all day with you,

Which brings me to this;

"If you can't take it with you, what's the point of

having it in the first place?"

Lord you are my Rock,

I am cenacle by nature,

"Smack me, and I'll smack you back, for less than a

bucket of pig feet, and a side of grits."

Lord you know that I'll be first to tell you,

"You come through."

..

4308

ΑΨΑ

CHAPTER SIX

The Killer Bee Report

67.

Does it matter?

The go between.

Or even the in-between,

Most often too lazy to only how you see.

It better matter.

What I see,

Even through the in-betweens,

ΛΨΔ

Because I'm seeing the strangest of things,

And we act like it is truly unseen.

It doesn't matter if you don't get what I mean.

 "The go between.".….. 1827

68.

Good Morning,

It has been awhile, been going thru other motions, no different from yours. No complaints. Pretty much enjoying the status of the Presidential deal and the fall of Capitalism, and can only imagine what's coming next, for the Land of Oz. If you put your money on Jesus, just cause someone said "Just pray on it", you may find yourself smiting their advise. Economic

ΛΨΛ

Cleansing is real people, truly more damaging than Ethnic Cleansing, but if you really want to be a superstar by taking your clothes off, and playing cute, or wearing your pants hanging off your ass, playing cool by all means please do so. Other than that, I hope that everybody had a descent weekend, if not a quiet one.

69.

I mentioned it subtly,

And she got it precisely.

Then she said,

"Stay brilliant,

Stay out there,

ΑΨΑ

Stay loving,

Stay of a giving heart,

Stay angry,

Stay defensive,

Stay outside the box,

Stay close to a playground,

Stay funny,

Stay intuitive,

Stay in love,

Stay cenacle,

Stay thinking,

Stay covert ghetto,

Stay honest,

Stay with that voice,

ΑΨΑ

Stay uptown,

Stay intellectual,

Stay ahead,

Stay Battlestar Galactica

Stay self destructive,

Have your tea with Satan,

Stay subversive,

Stay wise,

Stay vigorous,

Stay human,

Stay not content,

Stay caring about all moving around you,

Stay forgiving,

Stay a patriot,

ΑΨΑ

Stay imperfect,

Stay in tuned,

Stay on top of revelation,

A book that seems to not bother nor hurt you nor

frighten,

Stay talking,

Stay a quiet savior,

Stay you,

Baby stay.

You are more than what I've ever been used to,

You are more than what most have been used to,

Rather they've come to understand you or not,

Likely not,

I love you,

ΑΨΑ

And if you ever played Elvis you'd be awesome,

Or even Donny Hathaway.

So stay amongst the living,

Stay among us,

Because I believe in you,

Even if sometimes we lack just saying so,

Anthony I thank you, for being you.

Stay, Brother Stay.

Just stay you.

Only God is in you.

Don't give up on us, or the rest of us."

Suicide was still best in the end.

Who knew?

When I grew too quiet.

ΛΨΛ

They all knew it was inevitable,

But I kept them waiting until no more.

70.

Morning,

Yep I'm going thru changes, which seemingly says nothing for my heart. More antisocial than I need to be, the truth is, that it all has a place where I think more and more less of all things surrounding my life, with little or no reward, or gratification. Even waking up in the bed next to someone is of course "Whom am I fooling?"

I guess I feel fine, but really don't feel the need nor urge to relay it, odd enough for me considering that I

ꓘꟼꓘ

used to enjoy talking about everything. The point has been made, as to what has been lost, little gained, and moving on only means looking to be content with the big picture. Don't know what wakes me up in the mornings, not a clue, and I don't take a second to think about it, I guess I'm getting good at it. And last, as for being a Father, it has been as a dream, even still, sometimes I can't determine how real he is, a blur, moved on from whatever outcome, as if saying anything changes anything. That is all.

71.
To all things possible,
Let them be,

ΔΨΔ

To whatever beginning,

Could never be remembered,

And as the same for the end.

I guess, "To get over it huh........."

Not all think in terms of being a

Human being first,

But only when it comes down to the

Nitty Gritty,

then they remember.

How tight the hold is really.

However, if we stopped playing and took it serious

for only two minutes out of a day.

The beginning and the end would surely be the last

thing on your minds,

ᎪᎯᎪ

It would sound more like,
HOW.

72.
THE LINE HAS BEEN DRAWN BETWEEN
THE RATIONAL AND THE IRRATIONAL.
PROJECT THE SIZE OF THE COLONY,
LEAVE THE DYING TO DIE,
THIS IS REVELATION,
THIS IS HELL,
THIS IS PROMISE.
LOVE IS NO LONGER OBVIOUS,
I COULD PUT IT UP MY NOSE, AND IT
DOESN'T CHANGE A THING.

ΑΨΔ

GONE SOBER,

BORN AGAIN,

THE SHIT IS STILL THE SAME.

STILL I ENJOY THE CODE AND CONDUCT

OF IT ALL

BEING BRILLIANT

MERGING INTO A BLACK OP WITH

OTHERS,

YOU ARE TO SEE THESE WORDS,

SCRAMBLE THE THOUGHT,

MAKE SENSE OF PUPPET MASTERS

SHARE INFORMATION,

HIDE SOME OF WHICH FROM YOURSELF,

DIE FOR YOUR MAKER,

ΑΨΑ

AS YOUR SAVIOR HAS,

OR HAS IT BEEN TOO MUCH TO BELIEVE

IN,

THAT YOU MUST GIVE UP JUDAS,

IN ORDER TO EVEN THE SCORE.

THE TRUTH VERSUS LOVE?

CAN ONE SURVIVE WITHOUT TRUTH?

WITHOUT LOVE, IS IT MENTAL OR

EMOTION?

WE ARE ONE SPECIES THAT CAN BE

AFFECTED BY ONE SUPER VIRUS,

IRRADICATED.

AND THE WORLD LOOKS NO DIFFERENT

ΑΨΑ

AND I'M TIRED OF TURNING AWAY FROM

THE THINGS THAT I BELIEVE IN.

THIS IS MY FOXHOLE,

OUT THERE IS MY PERIMETER,

CRAZY BUT BRILLIANT.

GONE SOBER,

DESTINATION IS THE TRUTH,

PRIVILEGDED BY OTHER THAN HOME.

A YELLOW BOY,

IN A LABYRINTH,

CONCRETE AND COLD,

THAT I'VE BUILT WITHIN THE PROJECT,

MY BIOLOGY

SATAN'S HEART,

ΛΨΛ

GODS INTENT.

MIMIC THE MIROR,

RE-EXAMINE MY POSTURE,

DON'T FALL ASLEEP WHILE DREAMING,

LEAVE THE DYING TO DIE,

AND APPLAUD THOSE WITH FAKE

BROOKLYN ACCENTS

LOVE CHILD OF CORNEL WEST,

THOUGH I'M STILL A NIGGER,

A MOTHER-FUCKA,

DESCENDENT OF SEQUOIA,

REMEMBER THE RED RIVER VALLEY,

I'D NEVER BE MAN ENUFF,

NOR BLACK ENUFF,

ΛΨΛ

EVEN WITH GOD'S ANNOINTING

SO IN THE MORNING I'LL GET A HAIRCUT,

SOMETHING A LIL MORE TRADITIONAL,

STILL WILL NOT PUT ME ANY CLOSER TO

MY SON,

BUT STILL THE ORANGE IS STILL RIPE

ENUFF TO PEEL,

SO SHUT UP,

AND LET ME PLAY WITH THIS FIRE FOR

YOU.

FROM THE LEVEL TO LEWD,

SHOULD HAVE DIED A LONG TIME AGO.

JUST WANTED YOU TO KNOW,

DARE YOU TO ASK ME OF MY DISGUST?

ΑΨΑ

DARE YOU TO ASK ME OF THE OMEN
THAT LURKS HERE WITH ME?
THE LINE HAS BEEN DRAWN BETWEEN
THE RATIONAL AND THE IRRATIONAL.
SO whose SOUL IS LOST?
WITHIN THE PIT OF MISERY?
SOBER,
AND I COULDN'T SEE IT ANYMORE
CLEARER,
NOR GET IT OUT OF MY HEAD,
WHICH IS WHY I'M WAIST DEEP IN PUSSY
JUICY PUSSY AT THAT.
BUT WHAT I YEARN IS HIDDEN IN WORD.

ΛΨΛ

A PLACE WHERE THE MASSES ARE NOT
LOOKING TOWARDS THE
SKY WAITING FOR JESUS TO FIX THE SHIT
THAT WE'VE CREATED.
HERE WE ARE IN THE MIDDLE OF A
REVOLT,
JUSTIFIABLE,
AND IN OUR FAVOR.
HERE MOTHERS DO NOT KEEP A CHILD
FROM THE EAGER FATHER,
IF SHE VALUES HER LIFE,
WE DON'T DANCE IN TRICKS,
ANY CAT WHO IS CAUGHT BUMMING FOR
CHANGE NEAR WHERE BOOZE IS SOLD,

ΛΨΔ

WILL BE BEHEADED.

YOU CAN BE GAY IF THAT IS YOUR THING.

BUT TRY AND TURN SOME ONE OUT,

I'LL KILL YOU MYSELF.

HERE CHRIST IS A PROFESSOR OF

AMERICAN HISTORY.

AND AS FOR ME,

I AM A RANCHER,

BEEN MARRIED TO THE SAME WOMAN

FOR 64 YEARS,

SHE IS GOD

FIVE CHILDREN,

OUR YOUNGEST IS 7,

ΑΨΑ

AND AT 140 YEARS OF AGE IS EQUIVALANT

TO 32 EARTH YEARS,

BUT I'LL TELL YOU ALL ABOUT THAT

LATER.

THE LITTLE ONE WANTS TO PAINT.

IT'S ABOUT TO GET MESSY.

MEN AND WOMEN DO INDEED DIFFER,

I WILL ADMIT THAT I'VE BEEN TRIED BY

WOMEN,

AND HAVE RESPONDED,

AS IN TICK FOR TACK,

TEST FOR TEST,

UNWILLINGLY OF COURSE,

BE BRAVE,

ΛΨΔ

GOD'S VENGENCE MAY VERY WELL BE
SUDDEN DEATH,
I KNOW THE LEDGE,
A HUMBLE AMATEUR,
CLUELESS TO THE DAYS TO COME,
AMEND THE AMISS OF THE CHURCH,
I AM THE BAD SON,
BUT THE VOICE IS ALWAYS WITHIN
REACH,
AND I'M ALWAYS LISTENING,
LEARNING,
BUT LOVE SHOULDN'T BE THIS HARD,
I FIND MYSELF THE ACCUSED OF THE
WRECKLESS HEART,

ΛΨΛ

THE TRUTH IS,

LIFE IS COMPOSED OF TEXTURES,

NOT AS SIMPLE AS TV,

AND TRUE,

I AM HOME SICK,

NOR CAN I GO BACK TO THE BEGINNING

TO CHANGE EVERYTHING,

LONG STORY SHORT,

WOMEN KNOW THAT I LOVE THEM,

AND IF THEY DON'T,

IT IS NOT MY PROBLEM.

LORD KNOWS WHICH WIFE IS RIGHT ON
EARTH,

EVEN IF I LEAVE FOR EUROPE,

ΑΨΑ

REASON WHY.

IT IS HE OR SHE THAT BELIEVES THAT

THEY ARE SAVED,

AND THAT I AM NOT,

THEY ARE RIGHT,

AND I AM NOT,

BUT CAN ANY OF THEM SHOOT AN APPLE

OFF MY HEAD,

BASED ON FAITH AND HAVING NEVER

PICKED UP A BOW AND ARROW?

BUT EVEN IF THE ARROW HITS ME,

FATAL OR NOT,

I HAD FAITH IN THE OUTCOME,

EVEN IF IT HURT LIKE A SON OF A BITCH,

ΛΨΛ

THEN I AWOKE, 2-STEPPING TO LONELY

TEARDROPS BY JACKIE WILSON,

WITH THE SEXIEST VETERAN HAND

DANCER IN THE JOINT,

BUT AT 20 YEARS MY SENIOR,

SHE WAS SPITTING IN THE FACES OF THE

CATS THAT SHE BELIEVED IN,

YOUNGER THOUGH.

I WATCHED AS SHE CREATED A

PLATFORM,

THAT WE BOTH WOULD BE ENVIED,

I TIED HER UP THAT NIGHT,

WE NEVER GIGGLED SO HARD,

ΑΨΑ

AS CLASSIC OLDIES PLAYED AS A THE
SOUND TRACK,
SHE SHOWED ME PHOTGRAPHS OF A
YOUNGER HER,
TALKED SHIT,
HAD ME ROLLING ALL OVER HER
APARTMENT,
I WAS IN THE 70'S WITH A YOUNG WOMAN,
ALL OVER AGAIN
AND THE REST IS NONE OF YOUR MUTHA-
FUCK'N BUSINESS,
AS SHE IS A BORN AGAIN,
AND BIT OF AN OLD SKOOL FREAK,
BUT NONE THE LESS A LADY

ΑΨΑ

OUCH!!!!!!!!!

SHE SAID THAT MY CRAFT IS VALID,

NOT TO THE SUCKAS IN THE BOX,

BUT TO BRILLIANCE OUTSIDE THE BOX,

THEN SHE PASSED HER BONG,

LIT WITH TRUE BUD,

SHE WAS ALIVE AND CONNIVING,

I WAS STONED OUT OF MY MIND,

THAT MUCH CLOSER TO GOD:

FOR I'VE SAUGHT, AND SEEN,

TO BE ABLE TO SEE.

AND IT'S NOT YOUR PROBLEM,

THOUGH YOU ARE TOO JUDGEMENTAL,

UNLIKE YOUR GOD,

ΛΨΛ

BUT BE CAREFUL OF FEWER,

BUT OF NEWER DAYS.

THE VOICES AREN'T THE SAME.

ARE WE SQUARE?

AND IF NOT,

TAKE IT UP WITH YOUR MAKER.

I'VE BEEN GIVEN A GREEN LIGHT,

AND A KEY TO WHAT IS NON SECULAR,

KEEP CHEWING THE FAT JACK.

I AM SAFE WITH THIS,

AND I'VE TAKEN MY MEDS ON TIME.

PEACE.

ልፀ ል

73.

Been yearning the escape,

The year now is July 12th 2117.

With things being the way they are,

I guess today would have essentially been a great day

in another life.

But we are dying instead,

Some faster than others,

But none the less, all our fate is tied the same.

I can't make it to the surface anymore like I used to,

Because my bones have gone too fragile.

The few picture books that remain,

ᎯᎠᎯ

Remind us of the look of trees, lions, fresh water,

cities, talk radio, Hoes, and niggas, cool cats,

theaters, seasons changing, spaghetti, and so on.

 Ironic how there are no egos now,

Too dazed to figure,

How this came to be without God's signature.

74.

FOLKS BELIEVE IN BLESSINGS,

SO DO I.

FOLKS WANT TO BE BELIEVED IN.

SO DO I.

BUT HOWEVER

SIX YEARS HAVE BEEN AN OBSERVATION

AYA

OF FOLKS EXPECTING TRUST AS IF THE
PRIVILEGED IS A MUST,
THEY DESERVE AND I DON'T.
YOU SEE FOLKS ARE MY WATERCOLORS,
MY BEYOND JAZZ,
YEP I'M A SINNER,
AND ENUFF TO KNOW THAT I LOVE IT,
AND HIP ENUFF TO KNOW THAT I LOVE
IT,
BUT WHEN A SPONTANEOUS IDEA HITS,
WHEN SAFETY IS A VARIABLE,
FUNKY SEA FUNKY DEW
DO YOU SEE?
I'D RATHER YOU SMELL IT.

АФА

AT ANY GIVEN TIME,

PRISON AND I COULD MEET,

NO JOB,

NO DEGREE,

SO IT SEEMS THAT FOLKS ARE MADE TO

BELIEVE.

FOLK FALL ASLEEP BEHIND THE WHEEL

ALL THE TIME,

AS IN,

I HAVE A DEGREE,

I DON'T STEAL,

NOR DO I CHEAT,

SELL SECRETS,

LIE TO COLLEAGUES,

ΑΨΑ

FUCKED A COLLEAGUE OR TWO

FUCK THE PRESS,

NOT ANSWER THE PHONE,

COVERTLY KIDNAP YOUR KIDS IN ONLY 30

MINUTES,

FOLLOWED BY A CONVINCING LIE.

SINCE YOU TRUST THE BABYSITTER SO,

PAY NO MIND TO THE RANDOM RUMBLE

WE BELIEVE IN MAKE BELIEVE,

AND THE THING DREAMS ARE MADE OF,

WE LAY IN SHALLOW.

I'VE GIVEN SUNSHINE TO THOSE LONG

AGO,

SWAM IN THE BLACKEST WATER,

ΑΨΑ

STILL HEAR FLOYD SAYING,

"WE DON'T NEED NO EDUCATION."

"WE DON'T NEED NO THOUGHT

CONTROL."

AND STILL MY FAVORITE LINE,

"IF YOU DON'T EAT YOUR MEAT, YOU

CAN'T HAVE ANY PUDDING!"

"HOW CAN YOU HAVE ANY PUDDING, IF

YOU DON'T EAT YOUR MEAT?"

HEARD IT OVER THE WIRE IN THE FIFTH

GRADE,

BACK THEM,

MELISA MODLIN WAS MY SECOND LOVE

CRUSH,

ΛΨΛ

HER PARENTS DIDN'T FIND THAT SHIT
CUTE AT ALL,
I WONDER WHATEVER CAME OF HER.
THOUGH I WISH HER WELL.
FROM A GANGSTAS LEAN,
TO A LUIS CIPHER TILT,
STILL LOVE IS OFF BALANCE.
WHICH HAS MADE ME A BIGGER FREAK
THAN RICK JAMES.

75.
Just what does matter to me or I?....
You do you....
The ladder has been made....

ΛΨΛ

Never taken away....

Heaven so near that even the ridiculous, stutter for something else....

Ooohhhhhhhhhhh it makes me wonder....

The spirit that looms in the trees is still an old friend....

Many will die alone....

Without changing their own road....

The essences of time forgotten by them....

And that's a good thing considering if you've ever been hated by one of them....

Sweet is that winding road....

Be rock enough to show....

Gentle enough to tear....

APA

Something about a small hand in my own....

While looking out the back door....

Full of Soho Glory....

Come on....

Who the fuck are you....

I really wanna know....

Being a Father to this small one....

Is like my own....

A pleasure that the dating game could never vomit

forth....

I thank her every day....

Different from the day before....

Without trying....

Everything is fine.....

ΑΨΑ

76.

For never minding the never mind,

When it all moves in direction of,

Not much for how it moves around me,

Leave me be till you say it is ok.

Crazy world,

No God wants to touch,

So it is joy to dig in my nose, and wipe it on

whatever is close.

I know the place all too well,

The slightest touch is harm.

I dig a nice ass, but see it for more than flesh.

None the less a nice ass.

Run along kid, you're bothering me.

ᎠᏆᎠ

77.

Using the light,

To remember cold cool places that carry evergreen,

The scent of pine that can to be tasted in the all

around.

Where the lights in the sky,

Are as God would dance.

No greater place for me is, except the womb of the

Yukon's garden.

Brilliant winters,

Hip summers.

Hence also I am isolated, there in the memory of

such a place.

Though I walk amongst the concrete,

ᎪᏈᎪ

I am still in the hills of the Yukon,

So be gentle with me,

It is I, neither fragile, coward or weak.

I've slept in those mountains,

Climbed their breast,

Repelled their backs,

Even seen and heard the word

Of a gospel not written, nor discussed

I know the place,

Warmer than the hearts of the Lowland.

Where quiet is kept, and a voice heard can be

understood.

Here is odd.

When. … Using the light.

ΛΨΛ

78.

It has been the best,

Plain and simple,

Gone is the cute and cool fancy.

Hey, by the way she's a Billy Paul fan.

Loves to talk,

Got jokes too,

We both are silly,

Without feeling like sinners,

And loves a laugh.

Suspicious behavior all in Jesus name,

Those days are over.

I could not ask for more.

That is the more.

ΑΨΑ

We keep smiles on one another's faces,

And the giggle lit.

Priceless,

Refuge.

I get to keep my pants,

And she loves her dress.

Lord a muse.

Girl you Rock.

79.

"To ever want of, or from", is a short story loosely based on the uneasiness of freedom, we all yearn (a need) for, and how we all make believe that we don't need from someone or of something. The act of rejection is an odd phenomenon as in to banish one from a tribe or herd, usually due to an act that is deemed to be unforgivable. I could correlate this into prayer; the need for God, and that God is also make believe due to the interpretation of one's own perceptions, somewhere along this line is where the multitude of God's so-called children are at odds with even their own neighbor or otherwise around the world.

I am speaking of billions of people that want to get to heaven, but don't know how. This is where the conflict becomes disease and where God does not exist, because it becomes personal as in vendetta as in I

ΑΨΑ

don't like you because of, and yet we make believe, only to think to believe, that there is something to believe in, expecting to be heard by God when you speak or pray towards it. It is possible to be motivated by the concept of Jesus freaks, wickers, hackers, code talkers, fat little boys and girls or even Black Sabbath to Alan Moore. Or is it easier to misinterpret the love that has gone into each word, chosen precisely. Nostradamus never mentioned the liberation of the Negro in North America, or justified their attempt at glory to also be an act of segregation as in Jesus wasn't Jew enough. Blond hair and blue eyes, even had Jews turning their backs to that jack. Then to go ahead to give the bro a makeover, paint him brown, give him an

ᎪᎮᎪ

afro or such groomed locks; all to make it easier to identify with, but no such thing closer to the truth, because it is all behind the walls of The Vatican.

The guessing game is dangerous, and you are in danger, more so today than 1987. Consider this fiction and that I don't love you, because it is you that taught me as a whole, though bitter, you know it better. Finding ones purpose is a profound thing, to be inherently fearless, yet remain noble towards your efforts. They're wrong about me in the sense that I never wanted to be famous, be loved, nor a holy man, but it seems to have turned out that way. It takes a heart to forgive; God is in the snowflake. There is

ΛΨΛ

more damage to a race of people in a film such as "Hair Show." Then for two people to exchange a few unruly words at one another, and never speak again, because an apology is not enough, nor is Love, but then again neither is Jesus. I often think back to how my life was while I was living in the Midwest, and the chain of events that ensued, from Dr. York's to the 5 Percent's doctrine, to the "Born Agains".

I've listened, watched and learned their similarities, be the same. Racist separatist one and the absolute same to one another, even if it is to smite their own, while not being open to any other discussion or opinion. Three different groups divided by their own concepts

ΛΨΛ

of divinity, for there is their civil war amongst themselves, while they are beautiful people, and I've missed them, but they know that I am not one of them.

Then before I knew it, giving most to family what they want most, for their own absence, as in "Yes I do enjoy chasing cars and biting tires". What's up, can I help you, and how are you still doing? Resume, who gave a shit really? Was the question to myself? Tea with Satan seemed to be a comfort zone, since I was so already different from them. "Are you saved?" as in, "Are you Christian?" happens to be protocol for women here, but hold on a second. When a mother

ΑΨΑ

from S.E. murders four of her own children and said that the children were possessed by demons, the devil or whatever, but all together sounds so familiar, that the devil didn't have anything to do with this upset, simply a heavy burden is more than enough, for any human being. This is how I can relate to this story.

I once heard that the people in your life, that either were the hardest, or are the hardest to Love, are usually the One's who need it the most. The truth has a funny way of creeping up on you, but Karen gets it, and to add to the illusion since brilliance lacks a black (Human) renaissance taking shape. I'm trying not to speak on hating any one thing, for your sake. I don't

ΛΨΔ

want a broken family, as my own was, now that I have an offspring. Will he have the same as I had, or worse. I'll dare not teach, or program him into believing, that he does not need a woman, or the falsetto of Christhood, nor that being independent as a male will only isolate him from his own, as human first.

You can lie to me, and it be truth, would you dare die for me, and it be truth, but the truth is, I'd do it for you. Now it rains, gather on the porch in amongst a slighter comfort of your own wish, dare not to consider me no one, or that any of this matters not. For riddle it is, thanks to you. A best friend will lie to you. Let's imagine not being lied to, because, that you

ΑΨΑ

can now trust, trust no one, there are no lies. You are the wall painted of color, yet blank/afraid. Anyone would want of you sexually first, new to you.

When I'm much more curious in just how Human we really are, while Christ plays a role of so much relevance, still why pastors and officials have their way with words, that the masses come around to believe in. "Obama" vote for him, for Dr. King's sake and that dream he had is in fact now reality. You all play a real role in Omega Man aka I am Legend, here again is where I thank God for Will Smith and Charlton Heston excitant being. Tomorrow is neither bright nor grim, but only our promise. Which ones oneness is

ΑΨΑ

desired for us all? Yours or mine, his or hers, thus is the will enough? I won't be lonely forever, but for the past six years, it has been the best thing for me, imagine that.

There is a certainty that comes with it. Make no mistake, that people do see it, rather they wish to or not, but the brighter side is that it prohibits me from being dazed or confused, but emotions are a different story. There is no end to Life's purpose when simply all one needs is a precipitous nature. This alone is an act of God. Tell me nothing else; the closer I listen to her, she hasn't mentioned that whatsoever. It is true that even the dead can give meaning to a life. Viagra

ΑΨΑ

and all its wonders, to get it up, when otherwise its limp. To turn a man on when he has been turned off for so long, while stress, or his job can't do this to a man. I heard a woman's story about how she tried everything to get the guy off. Even though he was on the pill, which really is a scary thought, or was the Ole G, turned off nonetheless. I'll never know his position, but I had to call Ole Girl. She said she'll call me back.

God and I had an argument today, a lovers' quarrel, I suppose. It is Her that has taught me all that I know, and that the greatest sin, is to sin, and to be able, or willing to damn Her as I saw fit. Because the true cowards try too hard to please Her to the point of

ΛΨΛ

where they become hypocrites knowingly. A true Hellion gives away themselves within their own extremes towards divinity, or solace. You can hear it easily in their talk, in their humor. The truth is that it is easier for them to reject God's own creations. Doing nothing, or talking out the side of their necks, than to challenge their pride by giving in to the unknown. "But you don't write for them anymore, do you?" she asked. "Not anymore" I replied. But I can't blame not a soul, even if their thoughts are a lil too small. They are my people, and I've missed them. I Love them with all the Greater parts of my own Being, but will it change a thing? I'll leave it to time. "To ever want of, or from"

ΛΨΛ

is a short story loosely based on the uneasiness of freedom.

It is innate in us all to see through a lie, though as adults we try to hide them. But only hurt ourselves in the very end, even though we still have the tendency to settle for less than, if it makes it all worthwhile as a Lie. Tis the coward and the fool, that takes these words too seriously, and last, I really do ask of Obama, because of he and his family's own reality. I really do need to concur your readiness for change. The ability to deny is much more powerful than ones faith, it'll drive you into believing something else, rather than knowing,

ΛΨΛ

what is. I wasn't going to say the words, but I'll be nice.

From understanding the struggles from the Colored perspective, both past and present, regardless of how mixed the bloodlines are. Voting for anyone else, without giving that faith a real chance to change an outcome for better or worse, your vote will say, "I tried, because I care." versus " Screw the Dream." This isn't about politics, or the plantation. Sadly that it does come down to race for many, both colored and whites that can't concur to a lil bit of change. "Colored we stand, Colored the many will fall." So does the clown really have any empathy, sympathy, or finite

ΛΨΛ

understanding? Or simply a dope feign? Nonetheless I
will not pass their fear unto my only child.

"Pickled Pig feet anyone...........................I'm
buying."

Peace.

In memory of

Jay Bee

Alonzo

Brink.

Black Mac

Smothers

Crabral

Sonier

Strong

ΔΨΔ

and Bihal.

Airborne…………….Made us strong, and just a lil crazy.

Miss those real Muth'r Fukas 1st, every day since; the rest is none of your business.

….

That is Love.

….

Credits roll over "The Clash" "Know your Rights."

Followed by "The O'Jays, Back Stabbers."

Fade to black.

ΑΨΑ

CHAPTER SEVEN

Dinner at the White House

80.

It is the end of quarter,

To stand fast amongst those right....

Is a willingness that I have learned.

And a privilege,

From a hand full of great influences

All still down range...

What do I intend to mean to man?

አፋ

Am I love as he doeth...

To mimic his tale....

Or to lay down a much more primitive Morse

code....

That a few will understand....

I fear not even the unknown....

For it is as a sunrise....

So full of aw....

That even the source of my own Eden....

Would stop the pain of a race, not yet alive....

Hereto I preserve our dignity,

To end with the uniqueness of each ones pain,

I am open about this.

I don't need the Pain.

ΛΨΛ

Nor being the out....

Danger is the illusion....

Yet fascinating....

That resembles a dream.

An orbital approach.

It is the end of quarter...

When little hands reach for me,

I am reminded....

When the homeless approach as if they've known

me all along...

I am reminded....

These pieces of testimony have never been for me....

Yet I'm very well understood....

ΛΨΛ

Even while a confederate flag keeps me warm at
night....

No questions are asked of this....

Just a series of assumptions do follow....

Well at least someone else thinks they have it all
figured out....

Man that Nigga done lost his mind....

He's a bitch….

He's angry....

He's weird....

I do hear them talking....

Started in the third grade....

When only a few white men know that I'm dancing
circles around....

ልФል

The bulk of my own people....

This is my reality....

And the only way for me to have some fun,

With no questions asked....

But I admit that being single does bite....

Nor is it the best thing for me....

Not where I come from....

And in closing,

It is the end of quarter.

81.

Lately the sunset has been a guide,

A return to home anew,

When I hear them say "I don't need a man."

ΑΨΑ

When I hear them say "I'm independent."

I grow weary for her,

I grow afraid for me.

A city that rivers Aids,

And man is largely responsible, or maybe not.

90 percent heterosexuals carry the disease,

If she doesn't need,

Then she'll watch and witness decay,

Maybe extinction.

And so the birthrate will decline,

But she'll be ok,

Because she has her independent code,

Nothing more,

Since Jesus was also only a man.

ᎪᏢᎪ

A man,

A man in which she don't need,

Sad,

I've never heard one woman of pale fathers utter

these words,

"I'm independent."

"I don't need a man."

Because she knows survival,

Smart.

Lately the sunset has been a guide.

I can recall,

"Children of Men."

"Pursuit of Happyness."

"I am Legend."

ꬺꮀꬺ

Only lately.

82.

Then she asked,

Does it hurt?

Are you leaning into not caring at all?

Then what options are left?

To forget the day and the month by noon

To say something and it doesn't come out right.

To be proud of you, and it not be enough.

I'm tired.

All I know is only six.

My work dictates a patriot,

ΑΨΑ

Not a Ken doll nor Hollywood or much more
twisted,

I'd sell my soul for a petty 15-year marriage solid,

They'll blow by surely, but at least I'd know
otherwise,

What won't be known at all, because of you?

Nothing is like it used to be.

Thanks for looking out,

Hold on,

"Did he just say?"

"You could be my black Kate Moss tonight."

Kanye West huh.

There is a priest hidden in here.

That only you'd rip into pieces.

ΛΨΛ

When in Hell, I ask the Devil,

But when I have nightmares,

Mary leaves her sheets pulled back,

"But would you." I asked her...............

But thanks for asking,

Since it does come at a time when,

I wasn't born to be a commoner,

Cast away,

To be crucified while you watch.

Lord don't slow me down.

I'm in disbelief.

And from out these shadows I'm coming,

Only for him,

A gentle exhale,

ΛΦΛ

A gentle hold,

A gentle cry,

She did give,

Head in my lap,

I didn't mind.

But I'd become a better man without her checking

her own progress.

Stop your crying I said,

It was you that taught me not to cry,

And to turn my heart into your own stone,

I understand.

It was my own blind devotion,

I do see where I began.

You've been made to believe that I am the enemy.

ΛΨΔ

Then she said nothing else.

I will not be taken alive.

And we both seem to be fighting to survive.

Whatever the "Right" may be.

However I do need you too.

What are we waiting for?

Give me something to believe,

Would you please?

Free I give you this,

For a fee

I could send 2 thousand or more into bliss,

All while not a single child less than 11 to18 is
permitted,

Hard to decide,

ΔΨΔ

An 11 year old does not hesitate to shoot you in the
face in some places,

Within imagination,

This world.

Define freedom girl,

Tell me please.

Without Harriet or Holiday

Would you matter really today?

No.

When both I have loved,

You're

I'm much more thirstier than you are.

I still can hear a young Angela Davis

echo.............

ΛΨΛ

Can you?

Then she asked.

"I should go home huh."

You have to work tomorrow?

Yeah.

83.

It could have gone wrong from the get go.

Whatever saved it still has me bordering confusion.

Moment into mistake,

I was surprised to see Dana attended the funeral.

This would ameliorate her somehow.

She's melting from meddling.

Practice to misuse,

ΔΨΔ

Worried she is.

Odium into dismay,

We all blow it sometimes,

Sometimes if not most times,

Resolution or reservation,

May turn into sub-human.

Too much emphasis on the ridiculous,

When not enough of the riddle,

When nearly too rigorous for even the non- grateful,

Dana is already a part of our click.

Two of us found her suspect.

When you lose someone, to whom is to blame

usually is smitten first.

Sure she's 1 of 3 new to the crew.

ΑΨΑ

Part of the plan no less,

Everything Japanese about her,

Not to mention that she makes a mean burrito.

What just happened?

None of us saw it coming,

No one is at fault here.

Call you in the A.M.

Ah-ite girl.

84.

WHILE HEARING VOICES,

THE DOOR STAYS SATURATED, DAMP.

AND THEN THE BOY SPOKE.

HE SAID,

ΛΨΛ

DADDY DO THE WINNERS MAKE THE
RULES
WHILE THE LOSERS LIVE BY THEM?
HE WASN'T HIDDEN FROM HIS OWN
INTUITION
THEN WHY SHOULD I DIMINISH HIS HOPE,
HIS QUEST,
HIS ANSWER TO HISOWN QUESTION OF
TRUTH,
WHAT IS A FATHER WITHOUT BEING A
FRIEND?
BOTH HE AND I HAVE BEEN RAISED
WITHOUT OUR FATHERS.

ΛΨΛ

YET STILL WITHIN THE TRUTH, WHAT DO
WOMAN KNOW OF US.
AND FOR ANY SUCH LOVE OF GOD WHAT
DO WE KNOW OF HER.
RICOCHET
TURN THE HOLY PICTURES SO THEY FACE
THE WALL.
HOW WILL THIS MAN BE JUDGED,
THROUGH DISOWNING HIS OWN
CONVICTIONS
FROM A DISTANCE OR NOT AT ALL.
IMPULSE OR IS IT REFLEX?
TIME WITHOUT HIM HAS BEEN NOT LOST
AT ALL.

ΛΨΔ

IF I DIDN'T SPEAK OF HIM,

RARELY ONE WOULD ASK.

HIS MOTHER IS STILL RUNNING FROM

SOMETHING,

BUT INSIST ON COVERING IT UP FOR

SOMEONE ELSE, AND HIS TWO SONS.

TO SURROUND THE LITTLE YELLOW BOY

IN THEIR WAYS OF PRIVILEGE,

A PRIVILEGE FAR LESS THAN THE GIFT OF

BREATH.

SHE CALLS THIS "MOVING ON."

A BOUNTY I CAN LIVE WITHOUT.

IT IS HERE IN THIS LINE THAT CONFIRMS

THE ORDER TO GO AHEAD,

ДФД

AS WE PLANNED IT,
TO LEAVE ALL BUT ONE STONE
UNTURNED.
"DAD I WANT TO LIVE WITH YOU."
I WOULD CONSIDER THIS BY THE TIME OF
HIS FIFTH GRADE.
HEARING IT THIS SOON IS A SHOCK,
AND A GLIMPSE INTO HIS OWN HEART,
WHAT WOULD HIS MOTHER SAY IF SHE
KNEW,
SHE WOULDN'T SLEEP FOR SURE.
THEN SHE WOULD CLING TO HIM
TIGHTER, AND THE PHONE CALLS,
WOULD BE MADE SHORTER.

ΔΨΔ

MOTIVE FOR PERFECT EXCUSES.

DAYS WOULD GO BY, UNLESS I CALLED.

"DAD I WANT TO LIVE WITH YOU."

OK I SAID.

BUT WE MUST BE PATIENT FIRST, AS WE
HAVE BEEN.

IT CAN BE MADE COMPLICATED,

AND IT MUST BE MADE FAIR,

HE DOES UNDERSTAND.

TO RESPOND TO THE NEEDS OF HELL

FIRST, BRINGS ABOUT THE LIGHT AT THE

END OF THIS CORRIDOR HERE,

THERE YOU'LL FIND AN ENVELOPE WITH

A SECURITY CLEARANCE IN IT.

ΑΨΑ

WITHOUT IT I DO NOT ADVISE WALKING

THE VALLEY THAT SHADOWS DEATH,

IF IT IS YOUR SON THAT YOU SEEK

FOR HE IS SAFE WITH A DRAGON, AND

SHELTERED BY US IN THE BOSOM OF A

HALLOWED TREE THAT BARES FRUIT,

BUT CAN'T SEE US, NOR HEAR US.

NOT US,

BUT YOU,

WHILE HEARING VOICES,

THE DOOR STAYS SATURATED, DAMP.

AND THEN THE BOY SPOKE.

MIC CHECK!!!!!!!!!

THE STYLE OF THIS SKILL,

ΑΦΑ

WILL TAKE SOME TIME,

TO DEFINE,

WRAP YOUR HEAD AROUND,

AS I MANIFEST.

THE RHYME.

"JUST KIDD'N AROUND."

"DAD I WANT TO LIVE WITH YOU."

THOUGH IT COULD VERY WELL BE A

FIGMENT OF MY IMAGINATION.

THUS THE REACH INTO THE DARK,

FOR ITS GROWL IS NOT OF THIS WORLD,

WHENCE YOU WILL BE MAULED AND

EATEN TO DEATH,

"OF COURSE IT'S GONNA HURT LIKE SHIT."

ᎠᏢᎪ

THAT'S THE SILLY PART,

THAT'S THE PUNCH LINE.

LITTLE MAN IS A PART TO MY WHOLE.

BOTH SO FAR FROM ADAM,

WHAT A SACRIFICE FOR A DREAM,

HE IS MY LITTLE BIG MOUNTAIN,

FOR HE IS MY SON,

WHILE I'M HEARING VOICES.

85.

If I could let it all out, it would sound something like this. Yep, still think about her, in dreams too, she shows up. Even touched her once on a pass by; on the shoulder of course. That was enuff for us both minus

ΛΨΛ

eye contact, she sees me while I'm not watching her, and I see her when she's not watching me, the usual I suppose. A little piece of inspiration, or maybe even a little piece of desperation, she happens to be a piece of strength, and if the sun refuses to shine I'd still love her as I do still.

Settling with her is not based on faith, but time or timing is more so. Yummy lil thang, so full of thangs that only cell memory can only recall, lord knows I still love her, but love isn't enuff within this reality, simply cuz we are guessing as to what it is to begin with. For the moment love is only a concept of he say she say, but however whatever I've come to understand about

ΑΨΑ

the phenomena I still find it easy or as I've done in the past, to drink more drink, and then push away of any dinner table that has an issue with anything other than small talk.

There is a quality about her that I have yet to see or recall from others, not even in the one that so calls spoils me now currently. Surely it had a lot to do with her angle on god as a woman, her no nonsense approach to divinity. Whenever a so called best friend recalls her name and hints me to email her a rude gesture, I smile and agree his logic feeding his envy/jealousy as if he too were a bitch or madly in love with me, as a possibility…huh. As he may very

ΑΨΑ

well be living in the closet and have that attraction to me.

Otherwise I can not conclude why as a grown man he would still say negative shit, or try to get me to say damaging things to her, cuz it aint cute nor cunning, unless he as well is a bitch, with a child and a wife/diversion/ now separated, but none the less in the maybe closet, and I'm not flattered, though the ladies seem to say that I should be, by some of his gestures, "he wants to be me". But I can't recommend the time I spend in hell.

ΑΨΑ

His life is, world is, so conditioned to an appearance of normalcy, safe, restricted, all together far too common, but still full of headache, hurt, faking it; lack of love, trust, doubt, self insecurity, and freedom, but I love the bro, since there is a time and place for everything. However it's a living thing and a terrible thing to lose, staying focused, I miss her and may never hear from nor see her again.

But still I question how small is the world really, or if coincidence plays a role as it is mentioned, but over a lifetime there is nothing like a father and child reunion.

It's only a motion away, thus avoiding any other delusions or confusions of anything else, "come on

ᏘᎯᏘ

now, and give a nigga some credit". So what I still love the girl, rather than just settle. To look over and over and over again, at a Stepford wife potentially…catch my drift?

She may never know, although the same in that we all are, everyone around us, tested her too. You see, I've not convinced not one person that I do know, that I too know. A pattern does reassure within the cultural/social phenomena, but so what. A mother that cattle prods her own daughter for discipline, is not only creative, but out to lunch…a hot mess.

ꓘꟼꓒꓯ

I too am a feminist, shady don't break my balls, its hard stuff planning a revolt against Mexico, while getting it's refugees across the border into safe havens with little Nicky, "being a man". Political leaders on both sides have lost American virtue, eating their young. Now Turkey is gonna get some, this is about to get testy, domestic spying, "what do you know about spying" …

Here in a country still stuck in the civil rights movement and the kids in my neighborhood don't play with each other, now does that qualify me to be a domestic spy? Blackwater alone can clean up the

ᎪᏅᎪ

country putting all liberals and niggas in check...can you smell it, praise the Lord, oh baby.

German ingenuity won World War II. Bitch, a killer superbug on the loose only means just a nasty nation, but hold on now, that's a part of that apocalyptic vision many pray for. Now what's it gonna be, the second coming of a messiah, or be my own messiah, a better father than my own, a better husband than my mothers, the stuff not usually made into gossip.
"Getaway" by Earth, Wind and Fire has been an anthem of my own even as a child growing up in Washington, D.C. and "I'll Always Love My Mama" by The Intruders was about my mama. Growing up thru

ΛΨΛ

the 70's was quite the experience. It is still a period in time that I embrace. I'm gonna lay it all out for ya suckas someday, "up dig."

As for the meantime, this is but a fragment of a journey, less interesting than the shores of Orion's Belt, where life comes together with one man's imagination. Where tea with Satan transcends fear for the usual metaphors, though a place where the ghetto fabulous plow their own fields, and where the children snitch on the born again, and learning astrophysics for fun, so why be careful of what you wish for, if you are the one making the wish, lest you fear yourself. Can I too die like Jesus Christ and live to tell you about it, or

ΑΨΑ

is a nigga straight cold tripp'n. One of those cool things from my youth was when the girls from the neighborhood and surrounding blocks would gather in the alley and cheer.

Clapping their hands and stomping their feet in unison, head rolling, hips shaking, lip service, echoing throughout the way, while shooting marbles off to the side, and the faint sound of Rufus and Chaka Kahn's "Tell Me Something Good" could be heard a street over.

The air was a lot cleaner then, and so was the water, when a crush on another was innocent, yet felt good to

ΛΨΛ

think about that girl. Until we grew up, now look at how lonely, worried and independent, we have been tricked into believing it's all for a greater cause, and how afraid we've become of one another.

So that even in the event of compromise, commitment other than to a pet, and that we have lost our motherfucking minds. Now there is this talk about the lack of fathers raising sons. Even without my own dad being there and guessing that his child support bill is around 8 hundred thousand dollars give or take, and no time served, but my uncles were there throughout my youth, even still. And no matter how I thought when it comes to my own son, and my own idea of

ΑΨΑ

family. I never saw the break coming, until the very last second was I able to reflect, rewind and fast forward to the end. Indeed it is a catch 22 when it comes to women.

Family, cultural differences, religion, girl friends, money, post childhood fantasies; snow white or as I call it "Barbie doll syndrome". Insecurities, down to her own declaration of independence as a woman, when a lot of them can't even cook, and furthermore, they have been tricked, or bamboozled into an ideology of a so call feminist movement used to separate from men, to fear men, even go so far as to smite them on chosen levels.

ᎪᏢᎪ

There is an issue with control and manipulation, and it's not funny. In the near future I do see a decline in the birthrate of babies being born amongst black people in America. Now laugh at that, just when you thought your Jesus was going to save you, when you can't even see how to save yourselves, due to the extremes of how at odds we are with one another.

If I could let it all out, it would sound something like this. Yep…I still love the girl.

86.
There has been a resurge in psychological operations on people of color. Its women, its men, and its

ΑΨΑ

children, the most missing, and soon the fewest to be born. This current trend within the present-day social woes is serving its purpose towards damage control. To ignore this trend would be equivalent to catering to genocide.

Due to the lack of intimacy, and the lack of understanding God, thus clouded by self hate, minimizing trust, love, honesty, kinship, closet lives, faith, pride, illusion, mismanaged relationships, passive aggressiveness, disease, and a misinterpretation of the book of Revelation. It would not be fair for me to dig a grave, and to lay waiting at the expense of severe insecurities, or even more reluctant to mind control, either one is "One dark ride." On a global stage humanity doesn't seem to be priority, thus I'd rather be dead than to bear the burden of waiting, while in fear, selfishness, the lack of intimacy and the delusions of judgment. However this summary may be read and concluded as a bias from a man, father, that happens to be of color, then try considering that your God moved the pen, deny me either way. There is no divine plan, only evolution.

Then again I could be overly/overtly cenacle. Is that my right? Or should I be held accountable? Considering what has happened recently in Myanmar does change everything.

ΑΨΑ

87.

In Memory of: Naeilah Franklin.

A few tears for you, and a few for, these times.

Some of us will not forget your presence or your

influence; I'll fulfill my part in your name.

"Touch and Go." by Ecstasy, Passion, and Pain is

Dedicated to you.

"Great footwork by the way."

 You rock.

Maintain a solid journey,

Stay Safe

Nothing ever dies, You Know the drill.

Stay U and Stay sweet.

Between family, friends and strangers, you are loved.

AΨA

With all the madness as it has been lately, I too will pause, so that I will not feed into what justice is, or what may come of it.

There will be Goodness for you and yours that will resurrect from this.
I'll keep a Light on it,
"Fo Sho Shawdy."
There are plenty of whales out there to surf,
Plenty of secluded beaches on the planet to roam,
U know love and not to mention,
Billions of stars to sit and fish from and if by chance you run into Dana and Stacy, they still may travel together; give them a hug for me please.

ΛΨΛ

Heaven must be missing an angel.

Take care Naeilah

Peace and Blessings.

88.

Lately,

1. O.J. and Rodney King
2. O.J. and Jena 6,
3. Great timing,
4. Lil women raped in a bunker
5. Why would Jesse say Obama is acting white...not cool.... Jesse

ΛΨΛ

6. White Americans buying sperm from Scandinavian countries all for blond hair and blue eyes

7. Civil Rights Movement, huh

8. Civil war between Dems and Reps or is it North and still South, Yankees and Confederates, Blue and Red, Libs and Conserve's

9. I can't get Baptized unless I join, huh

10. And the Lord said "Say Werd!"

11. Miss my kid

12. Will fly out 2 C him 4 Xmas, cut down a tree like we used to

13. An Old Friend said today "I'm proud of you."

ΛΨΑ

14. Big Brother is my friend

15. Met this woman a ways back

16. Just turned 50

17. I've been sober for 4 months give or take

18. She's a wine drinker

19. On her birthday, it has been along time, since I had to care

20. Gave me the car keys

21. Got her home.............................42 miles

22. Got her into a shower

23. Got her into something to sleep it off

24. Been awhile since I've heard someone else cry

25. I wonder if she would have done the same for me, without giving me grief

ΛΨΛ

26. She had breakfast in bed

27. While I work on new Works in the basement, she created a studio for me to do so

28. No..........she's no Sugar Momma

29. We ain't Freak'n either

30. You may not get it

31. Why would Jesse say that?

32. O.J. will get off..............set up for sure

33. Tea with Satan next Wednesday.... FYI

34. White and Black America

35. I feel as free as a border crosser

36. Why is that?

37. Would like to have another child in 2008

38. Grandmother made it out of surgery, lost a foot
39. A cousin just got married, was cool, even though Jesus didn't show up to change the Diet Soda, water, and Apple Juice into Wine for those that enjoy
40. Moving right along
41. Things are looking and feeling really good
42. Got the play
43. Lord U, have a strange since of humor...too funny, we'll talk later
44. Caught the garter from the wedding.... Now that was funny
45. New film in the works

ΑΨΑ

46. A prenuptial agreement is a must
47. Honor those who are still missing, past/present

89.

Wzup peeps.

All is well on my end, and staying busy to no end, as well. Some of you I haven't heard from, nor reached out to due to, "Life". There are a few things that look good and are in my favor. Get a Nig out of mom's basement and on to the next. Been doing a lot of hand dancing with the Ole skool'rs... timeless, to keep things in perspective, too much fun. I'm good.

90.

For example, before filing for child support, I was a father. A father the second Gage was born, and I've played the role of a Father since along with child support (money when you can), pep talks, gifts, jokes n laughs, emotional support, etc. If I fall short TOO short of moneys I would then face some jail time, but to whose benefit would this be, the child, the guardian of the child, or the taxpayers.

Definitely not the child or the taxpayers, I wouldn't see my son if I came off of paper via the courts, I would be denying my privilege, then as a dad, even if I concurred to all of the above, (money when you can),

ΛΨΛ

pep talks, gifts, jokes n laffs, emotional support, visitation rights, etc. Yeah his mom made it clear and the only thing constituting me being a father is that MONEY and INK ON PAPER. That is the sad part. God don't like ugly, so yahl hold on real tight....

It is not my fault that "Mother" is not in the Trinity, no matter how much church there is. It has not been a real issue for women to dispute. Why...not the time for me to go into it...

Would it be my fight along with her if ever she really wanted a just cause reason to fight about it, rather that fight takes her to Vatican City.......Yes. Cause not being included in the Trinity is a Hell of a Psychological trip

ΑΨΑ

if I may say, and it reads Father, Son and the Holy Spirit.... She is a part of that Trinity even if we dispute at times, it'll be nice if their preachers tell them the same, if media tells them the same, if I had just a lil help from you, little things will change, for the better between us. There is too much wrong with our picture as man and woman, and really if I live to see 5000 plus walk 1500 miles for food and shelter, cuz government let them down, only half will make it, not including small children and the elderly, and the men will not be the only ones to carry the burden...feel me. Katrina is reality, so is history, pick any chapter.

ΛΨΛ

Love you anyway Girl, all of you, even those behind bars.

And that's keeping them honest.

91.

Are Women even sure of what they perceive to want in a partner, or is Dating easier on their conscience, personally dating is dangerous, but then again I'm just a Man, with very little to say.

She can wear the pants, take them please, but only if she can bake a mean mac and cheese while following her grandma's recipe. If not she'll still find a way to get out of that too.

ΛΨΛ

Oh yeah...don't freak your friends
And that's keeping them honest.

92.

Where the Lord makes a way to lessen ones load,

Satan snatches up the remaining souls,

So harmonious how they both work so well

together,

Done without fighting,

Unalike Gods look alike.

You can't fool either one,

But you can be fooled however.

That's keeping them honest.

08/2007

ΛΨΛ

93.

WHEN HERE I GO,

LOADED.

HAVEN'T BEEN THERE,

NO SUCH PLACE.

NEED TO STOP TALKING TO MY PETS

THEY THINK I'M TRIP'N FOREAL.

DON'T ASK ME,

CUZ I COULD HAVE SWORN YOU ALREADY

KNEW.

LICK DEM LIPS HONEY AND ARCH YOUR

BACK,

WAIT, HOLD THAT THOUGHT, I'LL BE

RIGHT BACK.

ДФД

94.

Just 2 weeks ago, on my job, there was a meeting in regards to usage of Nigga aka The "N" word, while on the job. Now I'll consider anyone being a Nigga in a minute, surely if you are being a dumbass, regardless of your race. That's urban culture as I see it. Hell, now there are "The Red Neck Games", how bout that. Who's bitching about that, not my baby's mother's father, of course not. But here is where it gets tragic for the Black Experience. Personalized Jesus tags for your ride, "I AM SAVED", "DIED 4 ME", "BORNAGIN", etc. You've seen this Shit as well, big and fancy cars, trucks, and, SUVs. Black Folks I tell you what. In my 4 years of watching white America up

ΔΨΔ

close, while in the mid-west at one time, as close as they'll go to wearing their faith on their sleeve is a Fish symbol on their car, and that says enough, but how we love to show off just how lost as a collective we can be.

I am just a lil ashamed by this NAACP stunt, cuz as much as yahl love Jesus, surely He'd be a lil upset at how commercialized, and how marketed He has been made into at the expense of Black America, and would likely say NIGGAS GET ON MY NERVES.........
Imagine that.

It's the 21st Century People

ΑΨΑ

Pick more decisive Battles

Get over it and catch up to the rest of the world, if you are going to be here.

I love you, and that's all I'm getting at.

Stop playing that civil rights, stuck in the past B.S. AND BUILD OR DESIGN SPACE CRAFTS, DESIGN CONCEPT CARS, REDEFINE LOVE, SAVE YOUR MARRIGE, DO CHURCH TWICE A MONTH, STOP TELLING ALL YOUR BUSINESS TO THOSE THAT YOU THINK ARE YOUR FRIENDS, AND ENJOY A PIGFEET SANDWICH ONCE A YEAR. WE CAN GET A LIL TOO SERIOUS WHILE LACKING THE EXPERIENCE.

ΑΨΑ

95.

Well anytime you feel like taking the pain and
shoving it up your ass,

Please feel free,

Cuz I've never felt better,

The identity you seek has yet to be explored,

How you must consider the past as a slave,

The present and how you struggle to get away from
remaining to be the slave.

The beauty in this is, there is no blueprint towards
your future.

Can you really solidify your culture, and your
customs way beyond the slave?

And if so,

ΑΨΑ

You'd be looking at a totally different race and a new culture,

One in which not afraid to live nor afraid to die.

ᎪᏆᎪ

READER'S NOTES

АФА